# GOING NUTS!

David W. Jones

David Jones is Pastor of Orlando Presbyterian Church and the author of eight other books.

For more information on David's books, go to:
davidjonespub.com

For more information on Orlando Presbyterian Church, go to: orlandopres.org

On December 22, 1944, during The Battle of the Bulge, U.S. General Anthony McAuliffe received the following communication:

> To the U.S.A. Commander of the encircled town of Bastogne,
>
> > The fortune of war is changing. This time the U.S.A. forces in and near Bastogne have been encircled by strong German armored units. More German armored units have crossed the river... There is only one possibility to save the encircled U.S.A. troops from total annihilation... honorable surrender...
>
> The German Commander

McAuliffe replied:

> To the German Commander,
>
> NUTS!
>
> The American Commander

# ❧ Chapter One ☙

*A question that sometimes drives me hazy,*
*am I or are the others crazy?*
Albert Einstein

For the Romans, *genius* wasn't something you were, like Albert Einstein or Thomas Edison, but instead, *genius* was something that visited you, a spirit, a sprite, a fairy that came whenever it pleased.

The Greeks had a similar concept and called them *daemons,* not demons, haunting, terrifying, possessing spirits, but *daemons*, diamonds, gift givers, idea bringers.

The Jews didn't speak of inspiration from sprites or spirits but the *Spirit*, the presence of God, the Giver of Messages.

So, for a Roman, a Greek, or a Jew, if you had no inspiration, no message, no art, it wasn't your fault, but the responsibility of your *genius*, your *daemon*, or simply God, who just hadn't shown up.

For the Sunday sermon writer, this is little consolation for no congregation will accept a preacher who excuses his or her lack of sermon by saying, "Sorry, I had no muse."

Jonah was preaching on John 13, where Jesus washed his disciples' feet. Jonah hated feet. The idea of washing feet, especially a fungi infested foot of a man, was more nauseating than stimulating. Yet, Sunday was coming nearer like a tide, and Jonah, with only a void where a sermon should be, was stuck in the sand. All he had was, "When Jesus washed..."

Jonah left his house for the nearby Publix Grocery Store, shopping not for food, but for inspiration, looking for some way, some one, to serve and in serving, start his sermon. Some pastors try to practice what they preach, but Jonah often found the reverse was more helpful, he liked to practice before he preached.

As soon as he pulled into the lot, as if by divine intervention, as if a gift from the Spirit's providence, he saw a woman by her car with her hood up. Jonah parked his car and approached, "Having trouble?"

She nodded her head.

"Let me take a look," he said. He gazed at the engine. "Try and crank it."

She got into her car and turned the key. The motor rolled but wouldn't start. Clearly the battery wasn't dead which disappointed Jonah. A dead battery was all he knew how to fix.

He looked at the engine, hoping for something out of place, some belt or wire that was obviously loose. He walked to her window. She rolled it down showing another sign the battery wasn't dead.

Jonah looked at her apologetically and said, "I've got nothing. Sorry. Is there someone you can call? I have a phone." Jonah reached into his pocket.

"No need," she said. "I have one."

Jonah looked around the lot. No one else seemed in distress.

He grabbed a train of five grocery carts from the corral. He pulled the end one, and it came apart from the rest. He pushed it back into the others. He walked to the front of the line and shoved until the group moved out of dock and into the lane.

He walked to the back and then pushed the line toward the entrance of the store. The weight and momentum were hard for Jonah to control. The first set of double doors opened, and he leaned hard to turn the train into the other carts. He was about twenty degrees short of lining them up with the rest but he decided it was close enough.

Bringing the carts back was helpful but not near enough, not personal enough to satisfy him, not momentous enough to rouse him. Jonah stepped toward the second set of doors. They parted in front of him, 'Just like the Red Sea before Moses,' he thought.

He surveyed the front of the store and saw several cashiers at work. He walked over to the counter of a young girl who was sliding groceries over a scanner. All the baggers were busy with other cashiers. She was alone, and her groceries were piling up, so Jonah decided to help her. He grabbed a plastic sack, opened it, and started to bag the groceries.

'I know there is an order to this,' he thought, 'cans on the bottom, bread and eggs on the top.' He was filling his third bag, focusing so hard on the task in front of him that he didn't hear the clerk say, "Sir, what are you doing?"

She asked again, this time emphasizing the, 'Sir...'

Jonah looked up. "Huh?" he said and then repeated what he was hearing, "What am I doing?" He looked at the bags, rather pleased at how tidy and upright they were, "What am I doing? I'm trying not to break any eggs, mush any bread, or bruise any bananas. That's what I'm doing."

"Are you new?" the clerk asked. "Where is your vest?"

"Vest?" Jonah looked around and saw all the employees in matching vests.

He noticed his own clothes. When he was writing a sermon, he sat around the house in tattered pants and faded shirt, with no intention to venture out.

"Usually I dress nicer…" he started trying to recall if he had even brushed his hair that morning, then remembered the clerk's question. "New? No, I'm not new. I've lived here for a long time. I remember before this was a Publix, it was a… a… a something else."

"Do you work here?"

"Work here? No."

"Then what are you doing?"

Jonah realized he had jammed the super market machinery. The clerk was no longer running items over the scanner; the customer she was trying to help was holding her purse tight to her chest and glaring at Jonah; the clerks to his left and right had also stopped and were watching. He laughed. "This isn't going so well."

"Sir," the clerk said, "those are her groceries," indicating the woman across the counter.

Jonah laughed again, "I don't want the groceries."

"Then what?" asked the clerk.

Jonah laughed again, "I just want to help."

The clerk didn't know how to respond.

Jonah squinted to read the clerk's nametag. "Jamie," he said looking to her as if there was not another person in the store, "I'm just trying to help." Then he turned toward the woman buying the groceries, "And madam, I'll even carry the groceries to your car for you."

The woman didn't say anything but took a step backward, away from Jonah.

"What's the problem here?" said a new voice.

Jonah recognized the tone, on days in the pulpit when Jonah's inspiration fairy, his daemon, his muse, had not shown up, on Sundays when the Holy Spirit had been noticeably silent leaving Jonah in a let's-see-what-he'll-do-with-the-void experiment, Jonah took on a similar tone, a more authoritative, without-a-doubt, let's-see-if-you'll-buy-this-one-tone.

He echoed the man's voice, lowering his normal speech an octave and raising his shoulders, he said, "What's the problem..." then he caught himself and restated an octave higher, "What's the problem? There is no problem."

Jonah turned and saw the store manager.

The manager looked intently at Jonah, then to the cashier at his front and back who were standing still when they should have been checking out customers, staring at him, curious at what would happen, not wanting to miss an incident.

He felt pressured. "Sir, there is definitely a problem," the manager started.

"Look," Jonah said. "I'm just bagging some groceries. I got them in the right order, cans on the bottom, fragiles on the top." Jonah picked up a bag to show his work. The bag started to tear at the bottom.

"Too many cans in this one," Jonah said. "Let me fix it." He pulled a few cans from under the eggs and put them in another bag, then double bagged the first one.

"Sir," the manager kept repeating while Jonah worked. Jonah finished and turned back toward him. "Sir," the manager addressed him again, now noticing that his check out lines were backing up to the center of the store and even more people were watching, "this is a grocery store. If you need food, there is a Food Pantry for people without money downtown."

Jonah shook his head. "No," he said, "I see the confusion. I wasn't taking this woman's groceries. I was just bagging them."

"Right," the manager said. "You just…"

"Seriously," Jonah said.

"You just came in here today to bag some groceries?"

"Well, I didn't come specifically to bag groceries," Jonah said. "I came to be helpful."

"And you picked this store?"

"I live close by." Jonah pointed toward the front of the store, then reoriented, and pointed behind the manager. "That way."

"You picked this store and this clerk?"

"Yes," Jonah replied. "I looked around and thought this nice lady, Jamie, could use some help."

The manager looked to his clerk. "Do you know this gentleman?"

"No," she replied.

"Does she have to know me for me to help?" Jonah asked. "Look at her. She's got her shoes off behind the counter."

Jamie quickly shoved her right foot into her shoe. She was so startled that not until the foot was all the way in did she realize that it was in the wrong shoe.

"Her body language will tell you how tired she is. She is scanning with her right hand and supporting her body weight with her left. Her eyes are red, either she was drinking last night, or hasn't slept for..."

"Hey!" Jamie shouted in protest. "I wasn't drinking! I've got a three month old baby."

"She's got a baby!" Jonah exclaimed. He turned toward Jamie, "Do you have any pictures?"

She looked down.

He turned back toward the manager, "Besides, all the other baggers were busy. And she was alone."

He looked back to Jamie. "Do you call them baggers?"

Her head was still down. She didn't respond.

"Sir..." the manager tried to interrupt but Jonah was on a roll assuming his own preacher voice. "Roger," Jonah said reading the manager's name from his tag, "I don't have to know someone to be helpful, do I?"

"Yes," Roger said. "Around here, you do. You don't work here. You aren't an employee. And you haven't passed a background check."

"Roger," Jonah replied, "I'm not trying to work the meat cutter. I'm not computing the price per ounce on the little stickers you have on the shelves. I'm just trying to be helpful and bag a few groceries."

"Sir, you can't."

"Why not?" Jonah asked.

"Because," Roger replied more condescending than authoritative, "people just don't walk in here and bag groceries. People don't just walk in here and help."

Jonah looked at him and replied, "Maybe they should." Jonah looked at Jamie to see if she agreed. She looked down.

"Sir," Roger said.

Jonah looked back at him.

"If you want to be helpful here..."

"Yes?" Jonah asked.

"Then buy something."

"Buy something?" Jonah asked.

"Yes, go and buy something. In this economy, you can help this store, the employees, this clerk, by purchasing something. Any one of the cashiers will be glad to serve you. Buy something. And then..."

"And then what?" Jonah asked.

"Then go home."

Jonah exhaled and then shook his head. He wanted the manager to know that he found him disgusting. Shaking his head seemed much more civilized than spitting on him. Jonah turned to walk away.

Jamie spoke, "Sir?"

Jonah turned back. "Yes?"

"What is your name?"

"Jonah," he replied.

"What is your last name?" she asked.

"Thompson."

"Mr. Thompson?"

"Yes?"

"Thanks for trying."

Jonah smiled.

He watched as the manager moved on Jamie. Roger drew close and spoke to her in a shouting whisper that only she could hear. Jonah didn't have to hear because he was certain the manager was scolding Jamie for encouraging the eccentric old man.

Jonah walked deep into the store, down the cereal aisle. "Too many choices," he said. He went over to the coffees, picked out a breakfast blend, then walked back toward the front. When he exited the aisle, he saw Roger still patrolling the cashiers. He retreated back down the aisle, across the rear of the store, and then advanced slowly up by the desserts. At the end of the row, he opened the freezer door nearest him and hid behind the quickly frosting glass. He pulled out a half gallon of ice cream and pretended to be reading the calorie count while he peered out searching for Roger.

When Jonah's body temperature had dropped ten degrees and Roger had returned to his post behind the customer service desk, Jonah hurried to Jamie's register. He placed the coffee and ice cream on the conveyer and waited.

Jamie finished ringing up the man in front of him and gave the usual, "Have a nice day."

She looked up at Jonah. "Hello again, Mr. Thompson."

"Hello, Jamie."

"About earlier..." she started.

"Don't mention it," he said.

From the rack by the People Magazine and gum, Jonah took down a gift card while Jamie scanned the ice cream and coffee.

He handed it to her.

"How much do you want on it?" she asked.

"Fifty dollars," he replied.

She punched in fifty and scanned the card.

"Anything else?"

"No."

She rang the total. Jonah paid cash. He took the gift card from her with his change, then handed the card back. "For the baby," he said.

"I can't take this," she said shaking her head for emphasis.

"Look," Jonah said, "Roger told me I should go buy something so I bought something. I just didn't believe it would help you unless I bought something for you."

"I can't..." she said.

"Yes you can. You are a mother. Take this for your baby," Jonah said. "Diapers are expensive. I remember. Buy the good kind. The generics have more blowouts than a humpbacked whale."

"You're not kidding," she said. "But I can't."

"You can," Jonah said. "Buy something for yourself. I recommend the gel inserts for your shoes. They'll help your feet and your back."

She was quiet. "Mr. Thompson?"

"Yes?" Jonah asked.

"Thank you," she said.

"You're welcome."

Jamie bagged the ice cream and coffee and then handed them to Jonah.

"Nicely done," he said.

# ೞ Chapter Two ೲ

*What sane person could live in this world*
*and not be crazy?*
Ursula LeGuin

2:05 a.m. Eyes opened. Eyes closed.

2:06. Eyes opened. Eyes closed.

2:06. Eyes opened. Eyes closed.

2:06. "Nuts," Jonah said as he rolled to his back and stared in envy at the motionless ceiling fan.

"You know," he said, "it wasn't what you said, it was your tone. You spoke to me as if I was senile, crazy, an Alzheimer's patient. I was just trying to be helpful. No wonder no one comes in your store to help. It's amazing anyone comes in there to shop at all."

2:07. Jonah sat up in bed. He yelled at the invisible Roger for another hour.

3:12. Jonah uncorked a bottle of wine. Half an hour and half a bottle later, Jonah was on the couch asleep.

5:19. Jonah awoke with a plan. He brewed a pot of coffee, toasted a bagel, and then got in his car. He drove slowly, afraid that if he went too fast, a police officer might pull him over and fine him for the intent on his face.

5:46. Jonah drove into the Publix parking lot, crossed to the other side, and stopped near the dry cleaner. Sipping his coffee and eating his bagel, he watched and waited.

A few cars drove in, parked, and the drivers went inside. Then a white Ford Fiesta pulled in at 5:52. Jonah watched Roger get out of his car, retuck his shirt, straighten his tie, and walk across the lot into the store.

"You, son of a..." Jonah said as he wiped the remaining crumbs from the bagel off his face, then reached into his pocket and pulled out a paper clip. He turned it over and again between his fingers.

6:12. Confident that all the early shift employees were inside, Jonah drove over to the staff parking area at the street side of the lot. He parked and got out of his car hunching over, but then decided that impersonating Quasimodo was more likely to draw attention than simply walking, so he marched as upright as a guard at the tomb of the Unknown Soldier. Jonah walked between the Fiesta and the car next to it. Paper clip in hand, he slowly folded to his knees. His joints creaked and complained about the unusual bending. Jonah hummed the theme from Mission Impossible as he unfolded the paperclip. He unscrewed the valve cap on Roger's rear tire and used the paper clip to deflate it. He then crawled on his hands and knees to the front tire and deflated it.

Mission accomplished, he stood slowly looking through Roger's car windows toward the store assuring the way was clear. He hobbled to his car with his knees giving payback for all the bending and crawling. He dropped the paper clip and his keys, picked them up, got in his car and drove home.

Back safely in his house, he put a spoonful of ice cream in his cup and poured more coffee on top of it, laughing, "Who is old? Who is senile, now? Stupid manager." He imagined Roger after a long day, going to his car, seeing the flats, and cursing his unknown assailant. Jonah laughed again.

Then he heard the voice of Jesus.

"Love your enemies. Pray for those who persecute you."

"Nuts!" Jonah said, his satisfaction replaced by an overwhelming sense of guilt and shame.

Jonah sighed. He looked down into his coffee. The ice cream floated on the top in a cloudy blob. The blob swirled and reshaped. Jonah looked closer. "Santa's beard!" he said. His mind filled the gaps. The mouth of Santa opened in a scowl and said, "Jonah..."

Jonah leaped toward the sink and tossed the cup from three feet away. He heard it break and watched it spit coffee and cream across the counter.

Jonah paced.

He grabbed his coat and a hat then went to his car.

He headed toward the courthouse, but spotting the American flag, he drove into the fire station. The big red truck was parked in the driveway. A man was there, half torso into the engine, half out. Jonah approached. Coughed. The man turned to see him.

He looked at Jonah. Jonah looked back.

"Where is the Dalmatian?" Jonah asked.

"Dalmatian?" the man asked.

"I thought there was always a Dalmatian."

"Afraid not," the man said. "Can I help you?"

"I want to report a crime," Jonah said.

"A crime?"

"Yes, a crime."

"You know this is a fire station?"

"Yes, I know. I'd like to report a crime," Jonah said again.

"You get that I'm a fireman and not a cop?" the man asked.

"Yes," replied Jonah, "but don't you all work for the same people?"

"If you'd like to report a fire, I can help, but I can't do anything about a crime. You know about any fires, do you?"

"No fires, just the crime." Jonah reached into his pocket and pulled out a paper clip. "I used this. You'll probably want to bag it as evidence."

"Again, I'm a fireman, that making any sense to you?" Curious, the man asked, "What sort of a crime?"

"I let the air out of a grocery store manager's tires. I used the paper clip. I confess. I'm guilty."

"What did he do to you?" the man asked.

"He was rude to me. He talked to me like I am old, senile, and crazy."

"He talked to you like you are crazy?"

"Yes."

"Okay," the man said. "You know you're reporting a crime at the fire station?"

"Yes," Jonah said reaching out with the paper clip, "you want the evidence or not?"

"The Dalmatian might choke on it."

"I thought you said there is no Dalmatian."

- 20 -

"There's not."

"Okay," Jonah said. "Listen, if we're going to continue like this, I need to know your name. It's important to me to know the name of my confessor. You have a name, or should I just call you Mr. Fireman?"

"No need to be so formal, you can just call me Fireman."

"I'd really like to know your name," Jonah said.

"It's Henry."

"Okay, Henry. Do you perhaps have an air pump so I can go right the wrong I committed?"

"We do," Henry said, "but we don't loan it out."

"I don't want you to loan it to me," Jonah said.

"You don't?" Henry asked.

"No, I want you to go with me."

Henry looked at Jonah.

"I get off duty at 4:00. Come back then."

Henry saw a surprising number of people who came into the fire station either looking for help or a handout. Henry's usual practice was to make them wait or even better was sending them away to come back later. Most didn't wait. Fewer ever came back.

3:55. Jonah pulled into the fire station lot. He got out of his car carrying a grocery sack.

4:04. Henry walked out carrying the air compressor.

"Alright, let's go," Henry said pointing to his truck.

"You not bringing the Dalmatian?" Jonah asked.

"Nope," Henry replied, "a cat chased him up a tree, and he won't come down."

Riding in the truck, Henry said, "I've been thinking about you today."

"Really?" Jonah asked. "It's nice to be thought about."

"Are you...?" Henry stopped short.

"Am I what?" Jonah asked.

Henry said nothing.

Jonah helped him, "Am I crazy?"

"Yeah."

"Isn't everybody?"

Henry was quiet.

"Look," Jonah said, "I've known a lot of people through this life, and I have to tell you, in my clinical opinion, everybody is nuts. Everybody is crazy. Some people are just better at faking it than others. Certainly there are a lot of people who are more functional in their insanity than others, but everybody is crazy."

Henry was quiet. They rode together a bit longer.

"Listen," Jonah said, "if you wanted to turn yourself in for a crime but didn't want to get in trouble, where would you go?"

"I don't know," Henry said.

"Fair enough," Jonah replied. "If you wanted to find an air pump and someone who knew how to use it, where would you go?"

"I don't know," Henry said, "fire station I guess."

They pulled into Publix. Jonah pointed out the car. Henry pulled a few spaces away, got out, and grabbed the air pump. Jonah brought his sack.

The lot was full, crowded with more cars and people compared to earlier in the day.

Jonah was humming. "You know this tune?" he asked.

"Mission Impossible," Henry replied.

"Hum it with me," Jonah said. "It makes it more fun."

"I'm not a hummer," Henry said.

While Henry inflated the back tire, Jonah opened his bag and pulled out a bottle of Windex and paper towels. He started washing the windows.

"What are you doing?" Henry asked.

"Washing the windows," Jonah said.

"I know," Henry replied. "Why?"

"Atonement," Jonah replied.

"Okay," Henry said.

Henry finished the first tire and moved to the front of the car. Jonah kept washing the windows. Jonah noticed someone in a vest come out of the store, walk toward the cars, then turn and go back inside. A few moments passed, and then Roger came running out.

Roger yelled, "What are you doing to my car?"

Jonah waited for him to get closer.

"I'm washing your windows," Jonah said.

"Why are you washing my windows?" Roger asked.

"Because I don't know how to use the air pump," Jonah replied.

"What air pump?"

"Behold the fireman," Jonah said.

Henry finished the tire and stood up carrying the air compressor back toward his truck. He did not acknowledge Roger.

"Who is that?"

"My friend the fireman," Jonah said. "His name is Henry."

"What was he doing with the air pump?"

"Reinflating your tires."

"Why was he..."

"Look, Roger," Jonah said. "I was mad at the way you talked to me yesterday when I was trying to be helpful. I came out here this morning and let the air out of two of your tires. I figured if I let out one, you'd just put on the spare, so I let out two because then you'd be stuck, but then Jesus reminded me that I was supposed to love my enemy. Now, Roger, while I know you have never invaded my village or run off with my daughter, you are the closest thing I have to an enemy. I'm washing your windows because the fire station doesn't loan out the air pump, and I wouldn't know how to use it anyway. If I tried I might over-inflate them and they'd blow up, or under-inflate them and you'd still be stuck, so I got Henry to do the inflating...

"Get away from my car," Roger said moving closer to Jonah.

Henry walked from the truck toward the car, ready to put himself between Roger and Jonah if he needed to.

"Roger," Jonah said moving away from him around the car spraying the Windex, "I have to wash your windows. You see, if I don't Santa is going to come back in my coffee again. He'll say my name with that tone of disappointment, and I'll break another mug. And then all I'll have to look forward to for Christmas is switches and ashes. Who wants that?"

"You are nuts. I'm not going to tell you again, get away from my car," Roger yelled.

Jonah kept washing and kept talking, "Roger, I used to wash my wife's car windows. I washed them every week. It was an act of love. I washed them just so she'd have a clear view to look out of. Roger, she died. She died, Roger, and I miss her terribly, but I still have that car. I can't sell it. You know what's crazy? I still wash her windows every week. So, I have to wash your windows Roger. I'm sorry I let the air out of your tires. Not my greatest moment. I am ashamed. There is part of me I don't like. So, I have to wash your windows. I have to."

Roger said nothing. He turned and went back to the store.

Henry waited.

When Jonah finished, he looked at the car. Satisfied with the job he'd done, he picked up all his paper towels and put them in the bag with the Windex and got in the truck with Henry.

Henry drove him back to the fire station, humming Mission Impossible all the way.

# ❦ Chapter Three ❧

*A guy needs somebody - to be near him.*
*A guy goes nuts if he ain't got nobody.*
*Don't make no difference who the guy is,*
*long's he's with you...*
Crooks in John Steinbeck's *Of Mice and Men*

Jonah sat staring at his computer. He had emailed. He set up a Facebook account and didn't know what to do next, so he sat and stared.

He looked at the computer's router. He turned it over and copied down the numbers from the back.

He got his phone, dialed and waited. After pressing digits for English, routers, and technical assistance, he heard a voice say, "Hello, this is Jerry. May I have make and model number of your router?"

"Jerry?"

"Yes?"

"Is that your real name?"

"Yes. It is Jerry."

"Hmmm," Jonah replied. "Judging by your accent, I'd say that Jerry is highly unlikely to be..."

"Sir, may I have the make and model of your router?"

"Jerry, I need to be honest with you. For us to have a working relationship, I need to know with whom I'm working. If Jerry's not your real name, then I don't think we can establish the necessary level of trust."

"Sir..."

"Jerry?"

"Sir…"

"Jer-ry?"

"My name is Rajesh."

"Rajesh?"

"Yes. May I have your router's make and model?"

"Rajesh?"

"Yes?"

"Are you married?"

"Sir, I gave you my name," Rajesh said. "Now it is your turn. Please give me the make and model of your router."

"What about children, do you have any?" Jonah asked.

"Make and model, please."

Jonah hesitated but then relented, "Where do I find them?"

"On the back of the router."

Jonah gave him the numbers.

"What seems to be the trouble?" Rajesh asked.

"The trouble is," Jonah replied, "I'm not sleeping much lately."

"No, sir, I mean, what is the trouble with your router?"

"Nothing really," Jonah said. "There is this little blue light on the front. I've never noticed that before. Is it supposed to be there?"

"Yes."

"Rajesh?"

"Yes?"

"You don't know much about sleep, do you?"

"I know about routers. If there is a problem with your..."

"What about voices. I've been hearing whispers..."

Rajesh was gone.

Jonah pushed back his chair from the computer and walked into the kitchen. He poured water and grounds into the coffeemaker and waited. While the coffee was brewing, Jonah picked up his church directory. He looked through it. So many families, so many people that cared about him, but not one he felt he could call. He had dedicated his life to being helpful, and was quite skilled at it, but in being helped, he was a novice. He was worried because a pastor seeking support, seeking help, within his or her church community can have blowback. Church people like familiarity, consistency, and stability. That's why they sit in the same places each week and like the same songs. Any rumor that there might be something wrong with the pastor can send anxiety through a church like fear through a herd once a single gazelle notices a lion's head peaking up from the brush.

He put the directory down and poured a cup of coffee.

He put a frying pan on the stove, turned on the heat, took a couple of slices of bacon from the freezer and put them on to fry.

He got out the top to the frying pan, placed it on the right of the stove, and then took a plate and placed it on the left with a couple of paper towels on it to soak the grease. He pulled open the drawer by the sink, took out a small box of matches, looked at them, and then confirming his decision, put them next to the plate.

He sipped his coffee and watched the bacon cook. He turned the two slices over, gauged the grease deciding there was ample, then picked up the phone and dialed 9-1-1.

When the operator answered, Jonah said, "My house is on fire." Jonah gave the location, told them to hurry, and hung up the phone.

He turned over the two slices of bacon one more time and then pulled them out of the spattering grease to the plate. He mentally measured the distance from frying pan to plate and then moved the dish a little farther away.

When he heard the sirens, he took a match from the box, lit it, and tossed it into the pan. Fire leapt up. The blaze startled Jonah momentarily and he dropped the box of matches. The blaze was higher than he thought it would be, but it wasn't hitting the fan above the stove, and the flames were within the boundaries of the pan. He picked up the matches from the floor and threw them onto the counter.

The smoke alarms went off. Jonah hurried to the front door and opened it.

The first response truck parked in front of his house. The horn of the large fire truck could be heard approaching. A woman in full fire array and carrying an extinguisher rushed out of the truck and across the yard.

"Where's the fire?"

Jonah looked past her to the man getting out of the truck. "Where's Henry?" Jonah asked, "Is Henry coming?"

The woman smelled the answer to her question and followed her nose to the kitchen. Jonah moved out of the way before she knocked him over. Jonah hurried behind her. She raised the extinguisher and pointed it at the pan.

"Wait!" Jonah shouted. "You'll get that goo all over everything."

Jonah hurried around her, took the lid from the counter and dropped it over the pan covering most of it. Flames shot up through the gap. Jonah grabbed the tongs from the cookware canister and nudged the lid over the pan covering it and extinguishing the fire.

"Whew, that was a close one. I'm glad you were here." Jonah turned to see the woman joined by two other firefighters and heard another one coming in the house. As the fourth firefighter ran in, he stopped when he saw the other two. Before, they were all in a rush, now they stood, looking at Jonah.

Jonah smiled, "Where's Henry?"

"Henry's not working today. How did the fire start?"

"I was cooking bacon. Just a couple of slices for me otherwise the fire would have been bigger. Would you like a piece? Sorry I don't have enough cooked for everybody, but I can make some more. I have coffee, firemen," he paused, "and firelady. Is that right, firelady? Well, firepeople are supposed to like coffee. Anyone want coffee?" Jonah asked looking around the room. One fireman raised his hand but put it down when he received a scowl from the woman.

"Sir, how did the fire start?"

"I was cooking bacon," he said.

"The fire?"

Jonah paused, "Would you believe I was smoking?"

She looked around, saw no ashtray, no cigarettes, no lighter, but did notice a pack of matches by the sink. She looked at the stove. Through the glass top of the pan, she thought she could see the charred remains of a match.

She looked at Jonah and sorted through her choices.

"Okay, boys," she said, "we're done here."

She turned to Jonah, "Sir, please be a little more careful. I don't want to be back. If there is another fire anytime soon, we'll have to investigate how it started. Do you understand?"

"I think I do. You really don't want any coffee."

The team headed to the door.

Jonah followed them. "Hey," Jonah said. The woman turned to see him. "Where's the Dalmatian?"

"We don't have one," she replied.

"Pity," Jonah said.

Jonah watched the trucks drive away, then went back inside and closed the door.

Jonah went back to his computer and sat down.

He stared at it until the adrenalin rush subsided. He emailed again. He checked his new Facebook page, still no friends. He recited what remembered from Psalm 38.

*O, Lord, all my longing is known to you.*
*My sighing is not hidden from you.*
*My heart throbs. My strength fails me.*
*As for the light of my eyes, she has gone from me.*
*My friends and companions, they stand far from me.*

He searched for the website of a new community church down the street from his. They advertised a twenty-four hour prayer line. He called it.

"Hello, twenty-four hour prayer line, how can I help you find God's blessings for you today?"

"Who is this?" Jonah asked.

"Just another of God's prayer warriors here to help."

"Prayer what?" Jonah asked.

"Prayer warrior."

"Does this prayer warrior have a name?"

"I do, but I'm not supposed to say it. It's against the rules."

"That's stupid," Jonah said.

"It's so the person, me, I mean I, don't get in the way of your conversation with God."

"Well, suppose I wanted to talk to God and somebody?" Jonah asked.

"We have rules for a reason."

"Are there rules on what you can pray for?"

"Sure."

"Suppose I wanted to pray to win the lottery?" Jonah asked.

"We can ask God to bless you financially," the voice replied. "We've seen God do miracles with people's finances."

"Even ask to win the lottery?"

"We believe that people of faith can move mountains."

"And even win the lottery?" Jonah asked.

"Even win the lottery. Sir, are you a person of faith? Are you a believer? Do you have a personal relationship with Jesus?"

"My relationship with Jesus," Jonah replied, "is very personal. It is so personal that he harasses me daily."

"Harasses?" the voice asked.

"All the time. Doesn't he harass you?"

"Challenge, discipline, but not harass. Are you sure you have a relationship with the Lord?"

"Yeah, I'm sure. Real sure, but let's stick to this prayer thing. What about healing? Can you pray for healing?"

"Sure."

"Now, I'm not talking about some minihealing, I'm talking a major healing. Can you ask God for a major healing?"

"Sir," the voice said, "I can tell you about quite a few miracles that have come from our prayers."

"Big miracles?"

"Huge. God can heal anyone."

"Anyone?"

"Yes, anyone."

"So, we can ask for healing for someone who is really sick, near death sick, and God can heal them?"

"Yes," the voice replied.

"Okay," Jonah said. "Now we're getting somewhere. Now we are moving. On to the nitty gritty, the big cheese, the whole enchilada, the lottery above all lotteries."

"Sir, is there someone you'd like me to pray for?"

"Yes," Jonah said. "My wife."

"What's wrong with her?" the voice asked.

Jonah waited, pausing until he was sure the voice he had was listening, sure his attention was fully into the phone call.

"She's dead."

"Dead?"

"Yes, dead, in the ground, colder than Lazarus, cremated, ashed, and in the ground."

"I'm sorry," the voice said. "Sir," he continued, "I don't think I can help you."

Jonah paused, "Yes you can. You can if you want to, if you really want to, you can help me."

"What can I do?"

Jonah waited again, "Tell me your name."

"But..."

"Tell me your name."

"Michael."

"Michael," Jonah repeated.

Michael was at a loss for what to say. He had never had a phone call like this. There were no procedures for such a call, so Michael just sat, held the phone to his ear, and listened to the silence.

Jonah felt like he was being pulled into the phone, like he and Michael were suddenly closer together, sitting side by side. The silence that frightened Michael comforted Jonah.

Jonah took a breath, a loud breath that Michael could hear.

"Michael?"

"Yes?"

"Would you just sit with me for a while? You don't have to say anything, just be with me? I just need someone to sit by me for a while? Can you do that for me?"

"Yes," he said. "I can do that."

"Thank you, Michael. Thank you..."

# ❧ Chapter Four ☙

*Sit, be still, and listen,*
*because you're drunk*
*and we're at*
*the edge of the roof.*
Rumi

Typically, Saturday was Jonah's day free from church responsibilities, as long as he had a sermon. His mind still an empty void about Jesus washing feet, he headed to the church.

He sat in a pew, listened to his breathing, felt his heartbeat, looked for some inspiration from God, and after about twenty minutes, he slumped into a nap. He thought he heard a rattle behind him, in the Narthex, maybe the door. He dozed on.

A vacuum cleaner roared up the hall and into the sanctuary, startling him.

"Nuts!" he yelled.

"Sorry, Reverend," Diane said, "I can come back later."

"That's okay," Jonah said popping up from the pew, "I was just about finished in here anyway."

"Reverend, there is a problem in the men's bathroom. I'm going to mop it up when I'm done in here."

"Problem?" Jonah asked.

"Yes, there is a leak in the ceiling. You want me to call somebody?"

"I'll go look at it," Jonah said.

Jonah walked into the men's room to see a puddle on the floor and a brown ellipse in the ceiling tile above that was birthing a new drop of water every three seconds. Jonah's mind ached, if there was that much water in this first floor bathroom, there must be a flood upstairs.

The stairs creaked as he climbed to the second floor, his right knee responded to every step with a click of its own as if the two were communicating in some strange code.

To Jonah's surprise, there were no dark spots on the ceiling and no water in the carpet. He stomped around the floor, anticipating water oozing up, expecting a squishing sound with every step. 'How does a first floor bathroom flood without a leak in the room above it?'

He looked out the window to the flat roof of the connecting building. Churches like theirs that had added buildings through the years often had flat roof buildings as connectors.

He saw two different pipes coming into the building right about the spot of the men's room ceiling. He opened the window and stuck his head out to see a vent above him. 'Perhaps one of those has come loose.'

From his pockets, he took out his keys and his phone, placed them on a table in the classroom, and then slithered out the window onto the roof. Small pieces of gravel from the flat roof embedded into his hand. He rolled over and stood up, brushing the gravel back to the roof from whence it came. He checked the pipes and vent. They didn't seem loose but could use some caulk. He'd call the elder in charge of building and grounds when he got back inside and retrieved his phone.

While he was up there, he figured he'd look at the gutters because when they get clogged, they can cause leaks. Looking toward the gutter as he walked, he didn't see the acorns. His foot slid forward, gravity overpowered him, and he fell backward to the hard surface of the roof. He mentally checked his body. 'Nothing broken. A couple of places likely bruised.' He stood cursing the tree that dropped the acorns as he brushed the gravel from his hands again.

The gutters were full of a combination of leaves, acorns, sticks, water, and roof gravel. Jonah kneeled down and pulled handful after handful of debris from the gutter. The water was cold. It made the joints in his fingers ache, but he continued. He laughed at the sound when the blobs he tossed hit the ground, and he delighted in the running water as the gutter way opened.

He stood back up and looked at the empty gutter wiping his hands on the back of his shirt. 'I should have gotten my jacket,' he scolded himself.

He picked up a handful of acorns and tossed them one by one, first back at the tree they came from hitting it more times than not, then at the playground slide which was too far.

"It wasn't supposed to be this hard," he said. "Not now. Not after all this time. Am I doing something wrong? What do I need to do differently? Am I an insane preacher trying the same things expecting different results?"

Jonah listened. He heard nothing except for Diane's car leaving the parking lot.

"Gideon asked for a sign, and you gave him one. Moses asked for a sign, and you gave him one. I'd like a sign, a symbol, a hint that maybe this is what I'm supposed to still be doing. I need some word from you that you're not done with me, and that my purpose here isn't over. I'll retire today if that's what you want. I'll quit tomorrow if that's what you want."

Jonah listened again. He heard nothing, but he did notice the window. He looked across the flat roof and saw the window was closed.

He hustled across the roof, hands out keeping his balance so that he didn't slip on any more acorns. His reflection in the window grew larger as he got closer. The window was closed and locked. 'Diane must have closed it when she walked through the upstairs in her final check before Sunday.'

"Nuts!" he yelled. He started to kick the window but decided against it.

He looked over to the parking lot. He saw his car, and there was one other. He couldn't remember seeing it when he drove in, but he wasn't paying attention either. Often people met at the church to ride together leaving a car with no driver, with no one to help you if you were locked out on the roof.

'Maybe they are inside.' Jonah began stomping on the roof, up and over the classrooms and onto the sanctuary, "Hello! Help! I'm locked out! Hello!"

He stomped back down the sanctuary, then up and over the roof of the classrooms. By this time, he was breathing hard and had stopped yelling. He walked across the flat roof and then up the pinnacle of the next building scanning the grounds from the high perch.

Then he saw her.

Just below in the valley where two buildings joined together, her body was huddled together in a tight ball.

Jonah crept down the roof toward her. He wasn't sure who she was at first, but then recognized Amanda. He thought she was sixteen, but he tended to keep all the youth younger in his mind, he had trouble letting them grow up. Maybe she was older.

As he got closer, in her right hand she held a can of Pabst. Jonah could tell by her body twitching that she was crying.

"Well, Amanda," Jonah started, "I thought I was the only one to come up on the church roof to drink beer."

Startled, she turned to see him and dropped the Pabst. The can slid for a ways leaving a trail of foam, then turned and rolled the rest of the way into the gutter ending with a small splash. 'Have none of these gutters been cleaned out?' Jonah thought.

"Uhm, Jonah…" Amanda started but had nothing else to say.

He liked that she called him Jonah. That was a good sign. Only new people in the church called him Rev. Thompson, or Pastor Jonah, to everyone else of all ages he was just Jonah.

"Amanda, what brings you to the church roof on Saturday?"

She didn't respond. He realized he was standing over her so he sat down, careful not to slip as he did before on the acorns. He knew if he fell this time it would be to the ground.

"How did you get up here?"

"There is a tree in the back where the branches overhang the flat roof."

"I know the one," Jonah said. "It used to be full of acorns. Now they are all on the roof."

"You have to walk part way across the fire escape," she said.

"I never knew you could climb trees," Jonah said. "Tell me something else I don't know. Tell me why you're up here. I gather it's not to celebrate."

She waited. So did he.

He could hear her phone buzzing. She didn't answer it.

"I am pregnant," she said.

"Pregnant?" he asked.

"I was pregnant," she corrected.

"Was?" Jonah's questions came as gentle inquiry.

"I miscarried early this morning."

"Amanda, I'm sorry. How far along were you?"

"Six weeks."

"Do your parents know?" Jonah asked.

"They didn't. They didn't even know I had a boyfriend."

"Had a boyfriend?"

"He broke up with me ten days ago. He said I'd become too moody. How could I tell him when he only loved me in a good mood?"

"Hmmm," Jonah said, thinking more but keeping quiet. "Have you told anyone else?"

"Just Stacey."

"That's what best friends are for," Jonah said.

"She doesn't know about the miscarriage. My parents know now."

"Now?" Jonah asked.

"My mom heard me crying this morning in the bathroom and came in."

"How did she respond?"

"I don't know. I ran away. I came here. I wanted to go into the sanctuary but the door was locked."

"Pity," he said.

"I probably wouldn't have gone in, even if it had been open."

"Why not?"

"I don't feel worthy," she said.

"That's who the sanctuary is for, all of us, no matter where we've been or how we feel."

He heard her phone buzz again. Again she didn't answer it.

"What do you think your parents are doing now?"

"Looking for me."

"How do you think they feel?"

"Worried."

Her phone buzzed again.

They sat together. Amanda cried. Jonah put his hand on her shoulder.

She took a deep breath. "Jonah, can I ask you something?"

"Sure."

"Why were you on the roof?"

"Apparently," he said, "I was looking for you."

"Looking for me?"

"Yep," he said. "I just didn't know it."

She laughed.

"Amanda," Jonah said, "can I pray for you?"

He held out his hand, she took it with both of hers.

"Dear God," Jonah started, "here Amanda and I sit, on the roof of your church, a sacred space set apart for your glory and for the benefit of your people.

"I ask your blessing on Amanda. Help her body to heal. Help her heart and mind to heal. Be with Jim and Sarah who are worried about their daughter. Help them know how to be helpful.

"God, we also ask that you receive the small life that was inside Amanda into your care. We trust that just as you have the whole world in your hands, so too do you have us. Amen."

"Amen," Amanda repeated.

The two sat. Jonah thought about getting down. He thought about it again and tried the second time not to envision himself falling.

"How about I drive you home?"

"Yes, please," Amanda replied.

"How do you think we should get down?"

"Over the fire escape and down the tree?"

"How about I use your cell phone and call someone to let us in?"

She handed him her phone. He called the elder in charge of the building.

"Bob, this is Jonah. There is a leak in the men's bathroom, and I'm stuck on the roof. Could you come open one of the windows in the second floor classroom and let me back in?"

Amanda heard laughing on the other end.

"See you in a minute," Jonah said.

Bob let the two roof dwellers in. He didn't think too long about his pastor stuck on the roof with a swollen eyed youth whose runaway mascara marked her face like a raccoon. With Jonah, he had seen stranger things before.

Jonah got his phone and keys. On the way to Amanda's house, he called her parents to let them know he was bringing her home.

"Jonah?" she asked. "What if someone asks you about how a can of Pabst got in the gutter?"

"I'll tell them the truth," Jonah said.

"The truth?" she asked.

"I'll tell them it slid for a foot and a half leaving a trail of foam, then rolled the rest of the way."

"What if someone asks you how it got on the roof?"

"Oh," said Jonah, "that's nobody's business but yours and mine. Besides, there's nothing to worry about."

"Why?"

"Apparently nobody checks those gutters anyway."

# ℭ Chapter Five ℘

*You may be right.*
*I may be crazy.*
*But it just may be a lunatic*
*you're looking for.*
Billy Joel

"Do you smell smoke?" Jonah asked Cheryl, the church's seminary intern. He was looking at Jimmy, age ten, being shoved by his older brother through the door into the sanctuary.

"Do you smell smoke?" Jonah turned to Cheryl and asked again, loud enough to be heard. They were sitting in the front pew of the sanctuary, the service was about to begin, the organ prelude was quickly approaching its conclusion.

"Do you think the church is on fire?" Cheryl asked.

"No, Jonah replied. "You know, smoke, cigarette smoke. Someone's smoking."

Cheryl took a breath. "You ready to get started?"

Without waiting for an answer Cheryl left their pew and went to the pulpit, careful not to trip on her robe. "Welcome...," she began.

Jonah stared and mumbled to himself, "I still smell smoke." Cheryl went through the list.

Jonah no longer paid attention to announcements. He once was the source for all things church, what met when and where and who was in charge. But now, he no longer even paid attention to announcements.

"You shouldn't smoke in the sanctuary," he whispered.

Through the prayers, the first hymn, the children's sermon, Jonah just sat.

"Nuts," he said to himself.

Jonah's turn came. He walked to the podium and opened the Bible. He thought maybe an old sermon would come to him, something he'd done a few times, in different locations, the mode, the mood, the words would just come. They didn't.

Jonah cleared his throat, "Ahem. Our text for today." He knew the bulletin had the scripture as John 13:1-16.

He turned past it.

He still didn't have a sermon on Jesus washing feet. He turned the page over and looked down, "Our scripture this morning is," he waited for his eyes to focus, "John 14. Jesus said, 'I'm going to prepare a place for you...'" He could hear his voice, the tone, the rhythm, but not the words.

He looked out onto the congregation. He saw ten year old Jimmy sitting with his family.

"I remember ten," Jonah said and then realized his sermon had begun. Raspy voiced, Jonah continued. He simply described what he saw.

"Ten years old. Sitting in our family car. Staring ahead. Sandwiched between my father, a giant of a man, six feet three inches, over two hundred pounds, and to my right, my brother-in-law, a mountain of a man, shorter than my father, shorter and wider.

"In front of me is the car's a.m. radio. But it's not on. My father likes the quiet.

"My sister's hand is on my shoulder. My two sisters and mother are riding in the back seat. I lean back and give it a little peck. Then I realize it's not my sister's hand I had kissed, but my oversized brother-in-law's paw. The hair gave it away.

"'How much longer?' I ask squirming so much at this point that I tip my father's hand holding his cup of coffee and it spills a little. My father growls at me giving no more answer than his displeasure.

"When I'm older, I will ride nineteen hours from the coast of South Carolina to upper Michigan... I will travel twenty hours from deep South Carolina to a small town in Germany... I will travel twenty-four hours from Atlanta, Georgia to Hong Kong... but no trip in my future life will ever be as long as this four hour trek to Grandma's house. And what makes this journey so very long is that of the six people in the car, I'm the only one that doesn't smoke.

"I look at the road, and I think ahead. I know what is waiting for me when the car pulls in the driveway. I know my grandmother has prepared a place for me. She knows I am coming. In the small refrigerator in her house, the one with the pull down handle, there are two shelves of six and one half ounce Coca-Cola bottles, just for me. I know what's ahead. I will get there. Hug my grandmother. Get a pink lipstick lip tattoo on my cheek. Then I will run inside, grab the opener, and pop open my little bottle of joy. The bubbles will tickle my nose. The icy Coke will choke me as it goes down, burning all the way until it resurfaces through my nose. I will cough and drink some more. Glory."

Jonah coughed and looked out from the pulpit. The faces staring back weren't family. There was no a.m. radio, no dashboard, only faces.

He looked down at the Bible. The words in red stood out. "I'm going to prepare a place for you."

He realized where he was and when. He was not ten, but ten plus sixty-five. He was not in a car. He was in a sanctuary. He was not a little boy with his family. His grandparents and parents had since died. So had his wife of almost fifty years. His children had children of their own.

He looked out at the congregation and stared. Then down again to the words in red, "I'm going to prepare a place for you."

"Heaven," Jonah said, "must be like that. Six and a half ounce Coca-Cola in a refrigerator with a pull down handle." He closed the Bible, and said, "Let us pray."

He started reciting the 23$^{rd}$ Psalm, though he had memorized more than one version, the King James was what he always returned to...

"The Lord is my Shepherd, I shall not want..."

He realized he was praying alone, "Say it with me," he said.

The congregation joined in,

*The Lord is my shepherd; I shall not want. He maketh me to lie down in green pastures: he leadeth me beside the still waters.*

*He restoreth my soul: he leadeth me in the paths of righteousness for his names sake.*

*Yea, though I walk through the valley of the shadow of death, I will fear no evil: for thou art with me; thy rod and thy staff they comfort me.*

*Thou preparest a table before me in the presence of mine enemies: thou anointest my head with oil; my cup runneth over.*

*Surely goodness and mercy shall follow me all the days of my life: and I will dwell in the house of the Lord for ever.*

"Amen," Jonah concluded and sat down.

"Nice sermon," people said at the door. "I felt like I was really there."

"Me, too," Jonah replied.

That afternoon, Jonah did his visits, made a few phone calls, thought about going by the store for some cold Coca-Colas in six and one half ounce bottles. Instead, he went home alone and uncorked a bottle of wine.

# ❧ Chapter Six ☙

*Ah, when to the heart of man*
*Was it ever less than a treason*
*To go with the drift of things,*
*To yield with a grace to reason,*
*And bow and accept the end*
*Of a love or a season?*

Robert Frost, *Reluctance*

"What are you doing?" she asked.

There it was. Her voice.

He had not heard it in so long.

He waited. He would not respond until he got the one thing he wanted to hear.

"Jonah."

He soaked in the sound. She said his name. He had forgotten so many things, like his father's laugh. He held onto it after his father died. Jonah tried to imitate it, but over time, he lost it. His mother's twinkle, that look in her eyes when he came home. Toward the end of her life, her eyes sparkled no matter who came into her room. He held onto that sparkle, but over time it faded and then was lost. The precise way his children, when they were infants fit into his arm, right in the nook, or on his chest... He'd forgotten.

For her, he had forgotten the precise feel of her touch, the warmth of her hand as she would roll over during the night and reach out her hand sliding it under the hem of his shirt and onto the small of his back to affirm what she believed, that he was there, and to profess to him, "I am here. We are not alone."

He tried to hold onto how that felt, shoving pillow after pillow on many lonely nights into the small of his back, but the sensation was lost.

But this one thing he held onto, this one thing time had not taken nor had he lost or let go, the way she said his name, the tone, the tune, the way she jutted out the J. He could still hear her.

So he waited.

"Jonah,"

"Yes."

"Jonah, what are you doing?"

"Nothing," he said as if he were eight years old and caught playing with his father's pocket knife.

"You were supposed to take them to Whitewater Falls."

She loved that waterfall. She made him take her by it anytime they were anywhere close to North Carolina.

"You know I never liked doing what I was supposed to."

"Jonah..."

"And I hate traveling. I'll get there. I said I would. Sometime..."

He stared at the urn. There in front of him, on the coffee table in the living room, the urn with her ashes. He had gone to Home Depot, bought a trowel, returned to the church, and unearthed her remains from the church's columbarium. He took sand from the preschool playground and filled the hole before covering it up.

"You promised."

"I know I promised," he said. "But I didn't say when."

"You were supposed to..."

"Supposed to?" he asked. "I've never liked, 'Supposed to...' You know that. After all, I wasn't supposed to outlive you. I was supposed to go first. You were supposed to last, to live on. It only made sense. You were so much more capable of being alone. You were so much stronger. You'd be so much better at this than I am. Who thought I'd live longer? I prepared for almost everything, just not this."

The house was quiet. His mind was quiet, except for the throbbing.

She spoke again.

"Jonah?"

He did not respond, only waited.

"Jonah?"

"Yes?"

"Remember where we would hike? Those hills around Radnor Lake? Remember?"

"Yes."

"Go there," she said.

He waited, hoping he'd hear his name again. He didn't.

He took his coat and hat, leaving the urn, her ashes, on the table behind. He walked slowly to his car and drove to the parking lot at Radnor Lake.

"What am I doing?" he asked himself the question he had heard before. "I know what I'm doing, I'm going nuts."

He started walking the trail, into the woods, around the lake. About half way, he turned away from the water and toward the hill.

He started upward. His legs were heavy. He picked a walking stick from the side of the path. Someone had used it before, most of the bark had been pulled off.

The sky was gray. The leaves covered the path. Later in the year, the foot traffic would crumble the leaves and the rain would at least clear them from the path, but now, in the winter, the leaves governed, they covered the ground and hid the path.

Jonah had to attend to every step, leaning more and more on his staff, looking downward for a roll or rise in the path where the leaves might be hiding a rock or stick he could trip over.

After a half hour of hiking, all he could see was the leaves. They didn't crunch or crack. It had rained a few days prior, so the leaves only mushed beneath him.

He wished he'd brought someone with him. Someone to talk to him, tell a story, tell a joke, lighten the air. But he was alone. All he could hear was a slight wind through the trees above him, his breathing, and the sound of each step on top of and into the leaves.

The higher he climbed, the lower his spirit sank. When he crested the top, he sat down on the bench that faced the vista. In the distance he could see the lake, though he took no notice of it. All Jonah saw was the leaves, leaves upon leaves, covering the hill and rolling over the ridge.

"Why am I here?"

He thought of all his losses that year. All his losses, that like the leaves, merged into one large, encompassing pile.

"This is no good," he said. "Nuts!"

He stood up. His knees resisted the early departure. He walked ahead on the loop of the path. It topped the ridge and then turned down back in the direction of the parking lot.

The fresh air and oxygen intake from the hike intensified his thinking. He thought of all he had lost, not just the previous year, but so much prior. His grief combined with gravity and the hill seemed to be pulling him harder and harder. It took all the energy he had not to fall forward, downward, over the leaves that covered the path. His staff had become more of a cane.

He stepped on until he came to another bench.

"This is no good," he said. His losses were massed together in his mind. 'I've got to pull them apart.' He set down his cane and picked up a handful of leaves.

He named each loss, and for each loss he pulled apart a single leaf and put it on the bench. He put a leaf for the death of his wife, a leaf for some friends who moved away, a leaf for his children that were all grown up, a leaf for loss after loss, separating them, each coming apart from the mass.

He breathed.

'I must do more. I have so much to be grateful for.'

He looked for some symbol, as the leaves marked his losses, he wanted some symbol for the joys in his life. He looked around, picked up a stick, broke it and started naming his joys. After a few sticks placed on the bench for friends and the church, he looked at the sticks next to his row of leaves. 'That won't do,' he thought. 'The sticks are as dead as the leaves.'

Then he looked up.

"Trees," he said. "I'll use the trees."

He looked upward.

"I'll use you," he said talking to the trees. "Sure, you're barren now, but there is life in you." Jonah could feel the life around him, dormant in the trees. "Sure, you look sparse now, but in a couple of months, you'll bloom, you'll canopy the forest, you'll rise toward the sun and sky in praise of life. You'll...live. You are my symbol."

Jonah touched the trees around the bench. He thought of one person after another, one possibility after another, one ability after another, one group after another, one activity after another, and for each one he touched a tree.

He touched every tree beside the bench and behind. He stepped on the walking stick, cracking it. He stepped back out onto the path and turned back up the hill. He climbed back upward. He started touching tree after tree, naming each one for something or someone he was grateful for, until, moving quicker, he just pointed to them, naming tree after tree.

He moved as quickly as his knees and his lungs would allow, climbing higher and higher, touching trees that were near, pointing at those farther away, naming each one, overwhelmed with gratitude, with life.

He reached the top, huffing, smiling. He looked at all the trees, all around him. He then saw what he had noticed but not seen before, the lake off in the distance. The surface was calm with a gentle ripple.

He did not sit on the bench but leaned against a tree beside it, feeling its strength, its life, its support.

Jonah recited from Genesis chapter one,

> *In the beginning when God created the heavens and the earth, the earth was a formless void and darkness covered the face of the deep, while a wind from God swept over the face of the waters. Then God said, 'Let there be light'…*

"And today," Jonah continued, "God said, 'Let there be life…

"Life," Jonah said it again.

Jonah recited Psalm 40, as well as he could remember it.

> *I've waited patiently for You, Lord. And you have finally inclined and heard my cry. You've brought me up out of my pit, out of my miry bog. And I will sing a new song…*

And then Jonah heard God's voice.

"Jonah, do you know what the difference is between you and the trees?"

He was confident it was God because God usually asked questions but gave no answers. Jonah didn't need a divine answer to this question, he knew it.

"Yes," he said. "The difference between me and the trees is that the trees let go of their leaves. I keep holding onto mine. The trees make room for new life. I don't."

Jonah sat on the bench. He cried for a while. He felt his grief wash from him and roll down the hill toward the lake. Jonah let it go. He held imaginary leaves in his hands and raised them to heaven. He prayed, "Here you are..."

Lighter. Brighter. Alive. Jonah walked back down the hill. The sun had set. The woods were varying shades of gray to black. The dark shapes of the trees were all around Jonah and he could feel them. He kept naming them, soaking into their life, their future potential, their immanent Spring.

The darker it grew, Jonah couldn't see the path as much as feel it, until he got closer to the lot, and the lights shined through.

That night, Jonah slept.

The next day, Jonah packed a bag, loaded an urn in the passenger seat, took his coat and hat and drove to North Carolina.

On top of Whitewater Falls, Jonah took off the top of the urn and poured the ashes into the river.

He said a prayer thanking God for their time together.

# ℭ Chapter Seven ℬ

*In a hospital they throw you out
into the street before you are half cured,
but in a nursing home
they don't let you out till you are dead.*
George Bernard Shaw

Jonah pushed the red button, the door unlatched, and he opened it.

'Odd that it's red,' he thought. 'Red is for stopping, staying out, not for going in. But here, you press the red button to enter.'

Jonah walked into the big room. He scanned the residents sitting in wheelchairs, staring at a television mounted six feet up on the wall. He turned to the nurses station, "Hello, Mark, Amy, is Katherine in her room?"

"Hello, Rev. Thompson," Mark replied. "She's in there. We haven't brought her out to the day room, yet."

"I'll go get her," Jonah replied.

"Sure thing," Mark said.

Jonah walked down the hall. He noticed several of the doors were decorated with pictures of flowers, butterflies, kittens and puppies. Katherine's door had a poster of azaleas surrounded by photos of a garden she used to tend.

Jonah tapped on the door and pushed it open, "Hello, beautiful," he walked in and then yelled, "Whoa!"

Katherine was sitting in her wheelchair wearing only a skirt, arms out stretched, free to the world. She looked at Jonah and said, "I'm hot. Who's controlling the air conditioning? How about bringing me some ice?"

Jonah had turned his head as soon as he walked in, but the image was branded in his brain. 'That's a picture I won't get rid of quickly.'

He stepped out into the hallway, "Amy! Mark! Anybody! Can I get a little help down here?"

Amy came at a quick pace. Jonah stepped out of the way. Amy opened the door and said in a voice normally used for a small child, "Katherine, again? And giving a show to the Righteous Reverend, you ought to be ashamed of yourself."

"I'm hot," Katherine said.

"I know you're hot, young lady, but you can't just go around casting off your clothes whenever you feel like it."

Jonah waited in the hallway until Amy came out. As he walked back in, Katherine greeted him with a big smile. "There you are," she said stretching out her arms toward Jonah leaning tight into the belt that tied her to the wheelchair.

"Hello, sweet Katherine," Jonah said, and he gave her a hug. "What say you and I go for a little stroll?"

Jonah wheeled Katherine out into the hall, toward the big day room, turned around and then back down her hall. He sang to her as they rolled along, "Oh, what a beautiful morning, Oh, what a beautiful day."

Katherine sang along, but some other unrecognizable song. "I love singing," she said. "Do you like singing?"

"I do," he replied.

The third time down the hall, Jonah's chest was feeling tight and breathing became arduous. The nursing home touched Jonah's biggest fear, being stuck, trapped, locked. He could only visit for so long before the claustrophobia started.

"How about you and I go outside?" Jonah whispered.

The nurses were away from the station. He looked down the long hall. A push of the red button will get you in, anyone can come in, but you have to know the code to get out. Jonah kept one hand on Katherine's chair and then punched in the code. He had seen the nurses let him out so many times he learned their hand movement without even knowing the numbers.

He heard the door unlatch, wheeled Katherine around, backed through the doors and out onto the sidewalk. Jonah started humming the theme from Mission Impossible.

He passed the windows of the day room, passed the windows of the physical therapy center and offices. He rolled Katherine down the sidewalk and next to a bench. He put the brakes on her wheels and sat down beside her.

"A bird," Katherine pointed.

"It sure is," Jonah marked. "Do you know what kind of bird it is Katherine?"

"Of course I do," she said.

"What kind is it?" Jonah asked.

"It's a pretty bird."

"Yes it is."

"There's another bird," Katherine pointed.

"What kind is it?" Jonah asked.

"A pretty bird."

"Yes it is."

"Speaking of pretty, that's a lovely red skirt you have on," Jonah said.

"Yes it is," she said. "I love red. Do you love red?"

"I guess so," if Jonah had a favorite color he no longer remembered what it was. Though he liked red, he couldn't imagine what it would be like to love a color.

"Katherine?" Jonah asked.

"Yes?" she replied without looking at him.

"Do you remember my name?"

"Of course I do, silly boy."

"What is it?"

"Hmmm," she thought for a while, "Tommy. Your name is Tommy."

"Katherine, my name is Jonah."

"Maybe," she said, "but I call you Tommy. Tommy. Tommy. Tommy."

"Okay."

Katherine started humming, pulling at the strings on her skirt.

"Katherine," Jonah started, "can I tell you something?"

Katherine kept humming.

"I feel like I'm losing my mental faculties, losing my memory, my focus. I forget things."

Katherine kept humming.

"The simple things are becoming complex."

Katherine started whistling.

"But I'm learning to be content. I'm learning to be okay, even now."

Katherine gave a long, stretched out, high pitched whistle.

A light rain started to fall.

Jonah took both her hands in his. He gave them a gentle squeeze. "I guess we better go back in," Jonah said.

"No," said Katherine, "outside."

"But Katherine, it is raining. You'll get all wet," Jonah said standing up.

"I want to get wet, God is giving me a bath," she pulled her hands from his and lifted her arms to the sky. She leaned her head back and opened her mouth.

Jonah did the same. He felt the rain on his face. He ran his hand over his cheek. It was rough; he had forgotten to shave that morning.

He looked down at Katherine. She was trying to pull off her blouse. He gently pulled her hands and hem back down. "Let's leave the clothes on," Jonah said.

She lifted her hands back to the sky. "God is giving me a bath," she said again.

"Yes, I guess so," Jonah replied. "A bath for you and me both. Just don't let it out in the congregation that you and I bathed together."

Katherine giggled and covered her mouth.

"You understand more than people think, Katherine."

Jonah raised his hands toward heaven. "Look at me," he said. "I'm Pentecostal."

Mark and another nurse Jonah didn't recognize came running up the sidewalk. Jonah pulled his hands down.

"Reverend," Mark said sternly, "you can't keep taking the residents outside. It's against the rules."

The other nurse undid Katherine's brakes and turned her toward the building.

"See you next time, Katherine."

"Bye, Tommy, Tommy, Tommy."

Jonah looked at Mark, "She calls me Tommy."

"No more going AWOL with the residents, Reverend," Mark said turning to leave. "See you next week."

Jonah gave them a polite wave but remained on the bench. He let the rain cover him, thankful to be outside.

"Oh, what a beautiful morning..."

He sang until he heard the question.

"What have you learned?" the voice asked.

"What have I learned?" Jonah repeated.

The voice was silent.

"I learned of a mistake I've made. A mistake I've carried my whole life, spoken about in sermons, taught about in classes, an expectation that has caused me great pain."

Jonah laughed.

"I've always sort of thought that life would... make sense."

"Doesn't it?" the voice asked.

"Not to me. Likely to you, but not to me. Yet, though it is not rational, it is relational. In that is the secret, if I'm going to stay sane, if I am going to keep any sanity in my remaining time, I've got to stay focused on others. Serving others will keep me sane."

Jonah thought back to the previous months, through his grief, through his pain. God had given him signposts along his way to guide him. God sent a tired grocery clerk, a friendly fireman, a tree climbing teenager, a topless geriatric, and more. God provided trees upon trees, so much life around him, so many people, so much joy, if he'd just be bold enough to reach out, to touch, to connect, to love.

Jonah recommitted himself to serving others, not because he was a saint, not because he was holy, not because he was righteous, but he would live for others because it would be how he would stay sane.

No matter what happened, he would use it for others, whatever pain he had, whatever loss he experienced, whatever became of his body or mind, he would try to find a way to use it for others. God would show the way. His pain would be his gift. He would do what he could and trust it was enough, to the end and beyond.

He hummed, then belted out as loud as he could, "Oh, what a beautiful morning..."

# ☙ Epilogue ❧

*Don't ask what the world needs.*
*ask what makes you come alive, and go do it.*
*because what the world needs*
*is people who have come alive.*
Howard Thurman

Jonah retired from the church.

His last sermon was on John 13, Jesus washing the disciples' feet.

Though he was no longer working full time, he was living very full days.

Once a month, at the nearby Publix, in the employee break room, inside her mailbox, Jamie would find a hundred dollar gift card. No one ever seemed to see the mysterious person who placed it there, though often, behind the shelves, out of sight, they often heard someone humming the theme from Mission Impossible.

In the Publix lot, quite often, Roger would leave work and get in his car. As he started the car, he would look through the windows and notice how they sparkled.

Jonah became good friends with Henry and others at the fire station. When someone came into the station looking for help, they referred them to Jonah. Jonah bought a Dalmatian and walked it by the station regularly. He brought it over when elementary school classes came for tours. Jonah and Henry spent a good bit of time together when Henry wasn't working. Henry taught

Jonah to fish, and Jonah taught Henry how to stay married.

Once a week, Jonah had dinner at Amanda's house. After the family meal, Jonah and Amanda would often sit and just talk, but sometimes they would just sit.

Jonah would often call the twenty-four hour prayer line and ask for Michael, and if he was working, Jonah would even let Michael pray for him.

And once a week, Jonah and the Dalmatian would hike up and around the lake. Jonah continued to name the trees as he and the dog each touched them in their own way.

# ☙ The Prayer of the Bible's Jonah ❧

from inside the Great Fish
Jonah, Chapter Two
(Paraphrased)

*I called out to You,*
*out of my deep distress,*
*and You answered me.*

*From the grave, from deep darkness,*
*I cried, and You heard my voice.*

*You threw me into the deep,*
*You cast me into the heart of the sea,*
*where the torrent surrounded me,*
*where Your surf,*
*Your waves,*
*crashed over me.*

*Then, I said, "I am lost, out of even the sight*
*and presence of God. I am truly alone."*

*The waters closed in over me.*
*The deep encompassed me.*
*Weeds wrapped around my head.*
*At the base of the mountains,*
*I fell into the deep where the darkness closed upon me.*
*I surrendered. Gone forever.*

*Yet, You pulled me up from the Pit.*
*My Lord! My God!*
*As my life faded, vanished,*
*I remembered You!*
*My prayer came to You!*
*My voice entered into Your holy presence,*
*where You heard me!*

*I am surrounded by others*
*who have fallen into the temptation*
*to follow after hollow, vain, empty idols*
*forsaking their true calling.*

*But I will live in response to You.*
*I will raise my voice in thanksgiving*
*for this life, this present, this instant.*
*I will give you each moment, as I promised,*
*because salvation and deliverance are Yours!*
*I will reach out to others*
*because they are Yours,*
*because I am Yours,*
*because this day, this moment, this instant*
*are all Yours.*

*Amen.*

# About the Author

David Jones is Pastor of Orlando Presbyterian Church
and author of the following books:

*Out of The Crowd*

*The Moment – there's no place like now*

*Enough*
*and other magic words to transform your life*

*The Psychology of Jesus:*
*Practical Help for Living in Relationship*

*Jesus Zens You*

*Moses and Mickey Mouse:*
*How to Find Holy Ground in the*
*Magic Kingdom and Other*
*Unusual Places*

*For the Love of Sophia*
*Wisdom Stories from Around the World*
*And Across the Ages*

*Prayer Primer*

For more information on these books,
go to: davidjonespub.com

For more information on Orlando Presbyterian Church,
go to: orlandopres.org